THE STORE OWNER

A Summer Job

A Summer Job

by Patricia Lakin
pictures by Doug Cushman

RSVP
RAINTREE STECK-VAUGHN
PUBLISHERS
The Steck-Vaughn Company

Austin, Texas

For Rick Robinson.

A Lucas • Evans Book

Published by Raintree Steck-Vaughn Publishers,
an imprint of Steck-Vaughn Company

Library of Congress Cataloging-in-Publication Data
Lakin, Pat.
A summer job / by Patricia Lakin; pictures by Doug Cushman.
p. cm. — (My community)
"The store owner."
Summary: Becka Alden helps her mother in the family's hardware
store and tries to think of ways to increase business.
ISBN 0-8114-8259-6
[1. Stores, Retail—Fiction. 2. Family life—fiction.]
I. Cushman, Doug, ill. II. Title. III. Series: Lakin, Pat. My community.
PZ7.L1588Su 1995
[Fic]—dc20 94-19720
CIP
AC

Printed and bound in the United States
1 2 3 4 5 6 7 8 9 0 WZ 99 98 97 96 95 94

"I am glad you and Daddy are letting me help you this summer," Becka Alden told her mother. She dumped a fresh supply of nails into the bin where they were kept.

Judy Alden was restocking the display of batteries. "Your dad did the same thing when he was young," she said to her daughter. "It's tradition. This store's been in his family for almost a hundred years."

"I hope we always keep it in the family," said Becka.

"You and me both," said her mother. "But business has not been good lately. The big factory in town has closed. It was our biggest customer. And the people who worked in the factory lost their jobs, so they don't have enough money to buy things from us, either. That's why our sales for the past few months are way down."

"Will our 100th anniversary celebration help?" asked Becka.

"I hope so. But the celebration isn't until next fall. Daddy is collecting old photos of the store for a special anniversary calendar. I hope the store can survive so that we can give those calendars out."

Becka loved the store. She couldn't imagine it with empty shelves and a FOR SALE sign on the door.

"I don't want our store to close," said Becka. "I'll try to think of something."

"Daddy is giving a speech today to the Better Business Bureau in the next town," said her mother. "He's trying to get new customers. He's telling people our history of friendly, honest service."

The cowbells that hung on the door rang out.

"My first customer!" said Becka.

"Nope," said her mother. "It's the delivery man. Hi, Joe, you remember our daughter, Becka?"

"Sure. Hi, folks," he said. "Here's the paint that Howard ordered." He handed the bill to Mrs. Alden.

She studied it. "I'll write out a check for $250."

"Wow!" said Becka. "That's a lot of money to pay out."

"Especially since we haven't been bringing a lot of money in lately," her mother said.

11

Joe Long held the door for a teenage girl as he went out.

"I hope she's a customer," Becka whispered to her mother. "May I help you?" Becka asked.

"Yes, please." The girl took a small sheet of paper out of her dress pocket. "I'll need some lumber, nails, wood glue, a pole, and some sandpaper."

This could be a big sale, Becka thought. "Are you building a house?"

The girl laughed. "You could say that. I'm making a birdhouse for my mother. She's still homesick for the Philippines. She loves nature, and bird-watching could be a good hobby."

Judy walked over to the girls. "What a lovely thing for you to do," she said. "I'm Judy Alden. This is my daughter, Becka."

The girl smiled. "I'm Maria Reyes," she said.

"Here are the nails," said Mrs. Alden. "They're sorted by size. Pick out what you need. I'll get the sandpaper."

"I'll get the pole and the wood glue," said Becka.

"Thank you," said Maria. "I also want to look through these craft books."

A boy walked in.

"May I help you?" Becka asked.

"My dad and I are going to put down stick-on tiles for the floor of my clubhouse."

Becka led him to the tiles. They were kept next to her mother's bookkeeping office, at the back of the store.

"These tiles are on sale," Becka said. "Only fifty cents each. What color do you want?"

"This blue is nice," he said. "I'll take a thousand."

Wow! This was a BIG sale. Becka wanted to scream. "That will be $500," she said, trying to sound calm.

"Oh," said the boy, looking at his money. "I only have about $50."

Becka felt her heart drop.

Mrs. Alden came over. "How are you doing?" she asked.

Becka bit her lip. "This customer needs a thousand tiles," she told her mother. "But he doesn't have the money to buy that many."

"What are the tiles for?" Mrs. Alden asked the boy.

"My clubhouse floor. It's about that size." He pointed to her office.

"This room is eight-feet-by-eight-feet," she said. "You don't need that many tiles."

"How many do I need?" he asked.

"Let's measure a square." Mrs. Alden gathered a ruler, pencil, and paper. "These tiles are twelve-inch squares. You need to cover a space that's eight-feet-by-eight-feet. That's sixty-four square feet," she said. "You only need sixty-four tiles."

Becka multiplied fifty cents times sixty-four. "That will cost $32. You have enough money!"

"Nice work, Becka," Judy Alden told her daughter, after the boy left.

But Becka frowned. "I wanted it to be a bigger sale."

Her mother smiled. "I'm glad you're taking our business seriously. But it's important to sell your customers only what they need, not more. That way, they will learn to trust you and will keep shopping here. Our steady customers are the ones who help to keep the store in business."

Maria walked over to Becka at the counter. "There's one more thing I need," she said. "Today's weather report warned that a bad rainstorm may hit here. I need to buy flashlight batteries."

"Do you want candles, too?" Becka asked.

"Great idea," said Maria. "I'll take two boxes."

Judy Alden looked at her daughter. "Very good thinking, Becka. That's the mark of a good salesperson."

"Thanks, Mom," said Becka. "And I think I'll make a sign for the door. I'll write STORM COMING, and I'll list what people will need—batteries, flashlights, and candles."

Judy laughed. "Terrific idea! That ought to bring customers into Alden's Hardware."

Then they heard a deep voice. "Did I hear someone say they want to bring people into Alden's Hardware?"

"Hi, Daddy." Becka kissed her dad hello. Judy Alden introduced Maria to her husband.

"How did your speech go?" asked Judy.

"Fine," Howard Alden told his wife. "I met some nice people at the Better Business Bureau meeting. They said they'd try shopping here."

"There is another thing I need," said Maria. "My father wants to change some light switches, but he doesn't know how. Is there anyone here who could tell him?"

"I can," said Mr. Alden. He put his briefcase on the counter.

"That's it!" said Becka jumping up and down.

"What's it?" her father asked.

"You could teach classes here in the store," said Becka. "We'd get lots more customers."

"Classes in what?" asked her mother. "Home repair?"

Howard Alden thought. "Great idea," he said. "I always wanted to be a teacher."

"Mom, too," said Becka. "She could teach people the math they need to use for building things."

"Another great idea, Becka!" said Dad. "Wait a minute."

He opened his briefcase, took out an old photo, and started to laugh.

"What's so funny?" asked his wife.

"History repeats itself," he said. He held up the photo.
"Here's a picture of my great-grandfather, right in this store,
showing how to use the new electric light bulb!"

"I guess good ideas just run in the family," said Becka.

Duties of a Store Owner

- Be helpful and meet customers' needs

- Order new equipment

- List and stock goods on shelves and in storeroom

- Keep records of sales and expenses

- Hire and train new workers

- Produce store sale ads

- Make future plans for store